AF059469

Mystical Magic

Mystical Magic

MAGGIE TAYLOR-SAVILLE

Copyright © 2021 Maggie Taylor-Saville.

All rights reserved. No part of this publication may be reproduced, distributed, or transmitted in any form or by any electronic or mechanical means, including information storage and retrieval systems, without a prior written permission from the publisher, except by reviewers, who may quote brief passages in a review, and certain other noncommercial uses permitted by the copyright law.

Library of Congress Control Number: 2022900250

ISBN: 978-1-956094-28-2   (PB)
ISBN: 978-1-956094-29-9   (HB)
ISBN: 978-1-956094-27-5   (E-book)

Some characters and events in this book are fictitious and products of the author's imagination. Any similarity to real persons, living or dead, is coincidental and not intended by the author.

The Universal Breakthrough
15 West 38th Street
New York, NY, 10018, USA

press@theuniversalbreakthrough.com
www.theuniversalbreakthrough.com

Printed in the United States of America

This book is dedicated to my late Husband

James Alfred Taylor 1932-2004

He always encouraged me to keep writing.

Chapter 1

Pain speared through her leg as she hit the ground! Dazed from the fall Katie rolled as Manfred, the seventeen hands chestnut horse reared up in fear before galloping away leaving her winded and trembling.

"Katie!" screamed her friend Jenny, as she wheeled her horse to jump off and run to Katie's side. "Are you O.K?"

"I think so" said Katie as she tried to stand up. "Darn Manfred!" she said as she gingerly straightened her leg. "I don't think I've broken anything thank goodness! She brushed herself down and straightened her riding helmet that now sat askew on her head. She was tall for seventeen, slim with short curly red hair and hazel eyes that now flashed as she looked around for her horse. "Come on" said Jenny, "I'll help you round up Manfred."

Set in a picturesque valley between two bays, the peninsular was the perfect place for horses with its lush paddocks and open spaces. Katie grew up with a love of horses but unlike her friend Jenny whose family lived on a large property, she lived in town with her parents and her Labrador dog Prince.

An attractive young woman, Katie was a volunteer at the local Trail Riding Ranch but only worked week-ends. At the end of the day she was able to take Manfred, out for a gallop and was the only one of the volunteers allowed to ride him. He was feisty but gentle and was her favourite. Belonging to Terry the ranch owner, he was not for public hire.

She loved this time alone, with the wind in her face and tendrils of red hair blowing out from under her riding helmet. Sometimes her friend Jenny would bring her horse over and they would ride the trails together. Jenny was one year older than Katie, also tall with blonde hair she wore in a long plait down her back.

This time something had spooked Manfred causing him to throw her. They rounded him up and Katie got him back to the ranch and squared away. The girls had been friends since starting school together in the small town of Lakeview on the southern coast of Victoria.

Jenny was able to ride her horse home but Katie who was still on her L plates had to rely on her mother to pick her up for her ride home.

Pasting a big smile on her face when she saw her mother arrive, she skipped a bit lopsided to the gate. Elizabeth, still a very attractive woman in her 40s, with the same red hair as her daughter but worn shoulder length, didn't miss much.

"What's wrong with your leg?" she said as Katie got into the car. Feeling guilty Katie mumbled "Oh I just fell over" Without another word Elizabeth started the car.

At home Katie called to her dog Prince. He came rushing around the side of the house nearly bowling her over. Once her mother had gone inside Katie breathed a sigh as she limped into the backyard to check Prince's water bowl.

She knew what would happen if her mother found out Manfred had thrown her. She remembered the arguments she had put up over having a horse. It was all playing over in her mind as she refilled Prince's bowl with fresh water.

Her mother had been in the kitchen preparing dinner when she had burst out. "Mum, why can't I have a horse?" Without turning around her mother had said

"Because we don't have anywhere to keep a horse." Ignoring this, she had reached over to pick up an apple from the fruit bowl.

"Oh no you don't" said her mother "dinner will be ready in a few minutes." Leaning against the bench, she had kept on "But mum, Jenny has a horse and she said I could keep mine in her paddock." Her mother had tried another tack. "Katie, we really can't afford to keep a horse." Without missing a beat she had come back with "But mum, it wouldn't cost much, there's lots of grass in the paddock."

Giving a loud sigh her mother had said "Katie, go set the table, your father will be home in a minute." That should have been the end of it, but she was fifteen years old and didn't know when to give up. She could usually get around her mother, but this argument seemed to be going down like a lead balloon.

After dinner while her mother was cleaning up the kitchen, she had tried the same argument on her father as he relaxed in front of the television. Dan was a quiet gentle man who wore a perpetual worried look. He was of stocky build, wearing glasses and with slightly balding hair. In his early fifties, he was a teacher at the local Secondary College and had perfected the art of hearing without the appearance of listening.

Without taking his eyes off the television he said "Katie, horses need more than just grass. What about feed, a blanket and a saddle. I'm sure you'd like to ride, so there's riding lessons, shoeing and veterinary bills" . . . She had overridden all these objections with a simple "I know Dad, but I could get a job." From the kitchen she heard her mother say. "Oh really!"

Katie had been determined not to give up and had pestered her parents every day for a week. Then one day, like the answer to a prayer, a notice had appeared in the local newspaper. It said, Wanted: Volunteers 14 years and over for Trail Riding Ranch. Hallelujah!

Her parents had talked it over and come up with the suggestion that she could volunteer, on condition that she stayed with it for one year and if she remained committed they would consider becoming horse owners.

Katie had been at the ranch for two years now and loved every moment she had with the horses, even the dirty jobs. She learned how to care for the horses, muck out and look after the equipment. She was also taught to ride. One of the conditions her parents had stipulated was, if she got hurt or injured in any way, it would be the end of things.

She had agreed to anything if it meant she could get a horse, so remembering this promise, she walked into the house with a big smile that she hoped covered up the pain in her leg. By the time the next week-end came around her leg was fine. She enjoyed working at the ranch. It was a tranquil place where the trails led through the trees and out onto the open plains that stretched to the base of the hills beyond. She had stayed on after her year was up.

Chapter 2

One day, she was helping saddle up a group of horses that had been hired out for a trail ride, when a sporty looking car pulled up at the gate. She gave the occupant a quick glance as he got out of the car, then turned back to her job, briefly thinking he must be one of the group going on the trail ride.

To her surprise, he climbed through the rails of the horse yard and came over to her. He was medium height, wearing jeans and a tee shirt that said 'If you love horses, I love you'. He shucked off his akubra revealing a shock of blonde hair that badly needed a cut. "Is the boss around?" he asked. He flashed a dazzling smile that showed off his even white teeth but it was his sparkling blue eyes that made her heart do flip flops.

"Um" she stuttered "H-he should be in the office." He gave her a brief "thanks!" he said as he walked towards the office, leaving her standing with her mouth open. He was gorgeous! Tall and blonde, she was smitten. Giving a big sigh she finished up with the horse and handed him over to the rider, then headed for the tack room.

On Saturdays, once the trail rides were organised and gone, she was able to take Manfred out for a gallop. She had almost reached the door when Terry, the owner of the Ranch, called her.

"Katie! Hang on a minute!" She turned around and saw him walking towards her. He was a real knock around horseman in his 50s.

Bow legged with a crusty exterior but a good heart. He wasn't alone. "Katie, this is Mike he's going to volunteer with us for a while.

Her gaze took in those brilliant blue eyes and she stood transfixed. She barely heard Terry as he said "Mike, this is Katie, she'll show you around." Suddenly realising Mike's hand was outstretched she reached out and felt a jolt as their hands met. "Of course" she stammered, again feeling like an idiot. She had never thought of boys as anything but mates, and feeling so awkward around this one was really throwing her.

"I'll leave you to it then" said Terry as he returned to the office. Pulling herself together Katie said "Come on then, I'll give you the tour." As they walked around the yards she got the feeling he knew his way around horses. He has to be at least eighteen she thought, because he was driving that sporty car. After a while she felt more at ease with him and by the time they returned to the office where she left him talking with Terry, they were laughing and on friendly terms.

Deciding it was too late to take Manfred out now, she gathered up her things and went out the gate to wait for her ride home. Sitting under a tree, she could see the sporty car parked in the shade and found her mind wandering to Mike and conjuring up various scenarios about him.

The next week-end she was busy mucking out when she heard the sports car arrive. She felt her heart thumping, but forced herself not to look up as he passed the stalls. He didn't see her, and she decided to keep busy so she wouldn't have to talk to him.

She couldn't stay there forever, and when she did come out, she was shocked to find him saddling up Manfred. To make matters worse, Terry was with him. She was incensed! She was the only one of the volunteers who was allowed to ride Manfred and she loved him.

Tears of rage burned and spilled down her cheeks. Who does he think he is she thought, I hate him and I hate Terry! She ran into a dark corner of the tack room where she rummaged through her things to find her mobile phone and called up for her ride home. If Terry thought she was going to stay, he had other think coming!

She got in the car without saying a word. Elizabeth sensed something was wrong, but since Katie looked like a thundercloud, she thought better than to say anything. The next week was a nightmare for the whole Richards family. Katie stomped around the house in such a bad mood that even her new part time job with the local Vet didn't improve her grumpiness.

Elizabeth felt like she was walking on eggshells whenever she tried talking to her, and poor Dan was totally confused, mumbling to himself "Hrmf women!"

Katie was usually up early on Saturday's eager to get out to the horses, so Elizabeth was very surprised to find her still in bed when she came out to the kitchen the next week-end. She went to call her, but the only response she got was a muffled "I'm not going, I hate Terry and I'm never going there again. I wish I had my own horse!"

Hmm, thought Elizabeth. Going back to her bedroom, she sat on the side of the bed and said to Dan, "Well I think I know why she's been so grumpy all week. Something must have happened at the ranch to get her so upset. She's always been happy out there. To be fair, I think we should look into buying her a horse of her own. She's done everything we asked, and she has volunteered longer than any of the others." Dan got out of bed and pulling on his dressing gown said, "You're right. I'll check around for a horse. In the meantime see if you can find out what happened out there." Elizabeth gave him a quick hug and went back to the kitchen to make breakfast.

Chapter 3

Katie didn't appear but they knew she would come out in her own good time. An hour later the phone rang. Dan picked it up and it was Terry wondering why Katie hadn't arrived. He was so used to her being the first one there, and had come to rely on her to open the gate and get things started.

Dan held out the phone as he called "Katie! Terry wants to talk to you." Grumbling she wandered out in her pyjamas and taking the phone, mumbled "Hello." Her parents tried to be unobtrusive but they couldn't help overhearing as it all came spilling out.

"I'm not coming and I'm never coming out there again!" A pause as Terry spoke then they heard her say, "Well it isn't fair, I've been working my butt off for over a year and I'm the only one you let ride Manfred. Now *he* comes along all buddy boy and you let him saddle up Manfred. It's just not fair!"

She banged the phone down and Elizabeth and Dan nodded at each other. Yes, it was definitely time! True to his word, Dan set about looking for a suitable horse for Katie and somewhere to agist it.

By a chance meeting with a friend, he learned of someone who was considering selling off a couple of his horses. Dan wasn't really into horses, so he talked to Elizabeth who realised they had been stalling about buying a horse, mainly due to her own experience.

At Katie's age she had her own horse, but in a stupid accident when her mount was spooked she had been thrown heavily and badly injured. She lay in a coma for a week and her injuries were severe. Told that she would never bear children, it had been like a miracle when she fell pregnant with Katie.

She had always tried to discourage Katie when she kept on about having a horse, for fear of her getting hurt. She longed for the day when her daughter would come in and say "Mum, I'm over the horse thing!" but she knew in her heart this was never going to happen.

Dan went to see about the horse, finding it was a lot more expensive than they expected, but Katie's eighteenth birthday was coming up and they wanted to surprise her.

The next few weeks passed all too slowly. Katie didn't go back to the Ranch. She had finished school at the end of the last year and had deferred university as she was working full time at the Vet Clinic. She was quiet and went about her daily chores without saying a word about the ranch.

Of course her parents said nothing about eavesdropping on her conversation with Terry, so even though Elizabeth was bursting to tell her about the surprise and see her happy again, she kept her silence. She was feeling quite excited knowing how thrilled her daughter was going to be.

Katie's friend Jenny was working full time now, which meant her days of horse riding moved to second place, and when a boyfriend came on the scene, Katie didn't see as much of her as before. Katie loved her job with Tom the local Vet. He was tall and lean with a receding hairline.

He was a quiet man and always wore a white coat. She had a way with animals and was looking forward to taking up her university option, and becoming a large animal Vet.

One afternoon she came storming home from work and went straight to her room slamming the door shut, leaving Elizabeth standing in the kitchen feeling like a mini tornado had just blown through. She moved to knock on the bedroom door saying.

"Katie whatever is wrong!" The door swung open as Katie emerged with the now familiar scowl on her face.

"Mum *he* was there!" she shouted, eyes flashing and red curls bouncing. "He who?" said a bewildered Elizabeth. "Mike! the one who came to the ranch and rode Manfred." Her mother waited for the rest of it. They never did find out what had caused the upset at the ranch, apart from what they overheard from the phone call that morning, months ago.

Katie couldn't tell her mother, how the sports car had pulled up outside the vet clinic and how for some reason her heart had jumped into her throat like a big lump. When the bell on the door clanged she had tried to hide in the back room. Unfortunately, Tom was busy and called out.

"Katie can you get that!" She walked out on shaky legs to face those georgeous eyes and devastating smile.

"Hi Katie!" he said, "So this is where you've been hiding. I missed you at the ranch!" Her heart was thumping so hard she could barely stammer "Er h-hello"

He didn't seem to notice, as he passed the order form across the counter saying "I'll pick them up tomorrow!" Without looking at the order, Katie put it on the spike for Tom and went back to her work. She was feeling very strange. Her palms were sweating and she didn't know if she wanted to cry, or throw up.

Finishing restacking the shelf, she called to Tom that she would see him tomorrow. On the way home she stewed over in her mind all the things she hated about Mike and what she would say to him when he came to pick up his supplies tomorrow. By the time she had vented her frustration, she found that she couldn't tell her mother anything. Elizabeth was still left in the dark but a knowing smile hovered on her lips.

When Katie arrived at work the next morning, she almost tripped over a large box that Tom had left near the door. Reading the docket stuck to the lid, she noted it was supplies for 'Wilton Stud' the largest horse stud on the peninsular. Skirting around it, she hung up her jacket and went to the surgery where Tom was sterilising instruments.

"Hi Katie!" he said as she popped her head around the door. "Sorry about the box out there in the doorway. Mike is coming to pick it up shortly." She felt her heart thumping as she said, "Mike?"

"Yes" he said "Tony Wilson's son. You would have seen him yesterday when he dropped the order in." Oh no! How could she have been so stupid she thought, wishing she could disappear into thin air as it all fell into place. No wonder he seemed to know his way around horses, and why he was so friendly with Terry. What she couldn't understand was why Terry had introduced him as a volunteer. She felt herself feeling angry again but this time her anger was aimed at Terry.

Her breath caught in her throat as the bell on the door clanged. "That'll be Mike now," said Tom.

Feeling like an idiot, was becoming familiar to her as she went out to the shop. This time an old utility truck was parked outside but standing just inside the door reading the docket was Mike. He looked up and smiled as he saw her. She felt herself blushing and quickly went behind the counter where she felt more in control.

"I was hoping you'd be working today," he said "When Terry told me you weren't coming to the ranch any more I was really disappointed."

Katie felt her hackles rising as she burst out. "Why did Terry tell me you were a volunteer? I was really angry with you and now I feel stupid." He moved over to the counter, and that made him much too close for her liking.

"I'm sorry about that Katie, but Terry wanted me to take Manfred out for a run because he was thinking of selling him and wanted my opinion."

Katie felt her heart drop and gasped with dismay! Reaching over to her, he said. "That's why Terry said I was a volunteer. He knew how you felt about Manfred and he didn't want to upset you."

She felt tears pricking the back of her eyes as she dropped her head to the counter, trying to hold back the tears but it was all too much. Mike was behind the counter in a flash holding her in his arms as she cried it all out.

When the tears stopped she was amazed she didn't feel at all embarrassed at find herself so close to him. Brushing the tears from her face she gave him a watery smile and said, "Sorry about that, I always seem to make an idiot of myself when I'm around you!" They both laughed and suddenly the sun shone again.

"Well," said Mike, "I'd better get going before the old man kicks my butt for taking so long, hope I'll see you around soon."

He picked up the large box as though it was light as a feather. She held the door open for him and watched as he tossed the box into the back of the utility and drove off with a wave.

She saw him around town a few times after that and her heart always fluttered whenever he waved or called hello. She had returned to the ranch a few times and Terry always let her take Manfred for a ride. She was glad he hadn't been sold. Although she kept an eye out for Mike, she never saw him there again.

Chapter 4

Elizabeth was happy to see her daughter bright and cheerful again. She seemed to have got over whatever the problem had been at the ranch, and chatted away like before about the horses, Terry and the other volunteers. Sometimes it seemed her mind was elsewhere and the name 'Mike' frequently came up in conversation.

Dan had been giving her driving lessons and on her 18th birthday she nervously went for her license. She got it first go, and they celebrated with a meal at the local pub. Dan was so proud of his girls who both looked stunning.

Elizabeth was wearing a long black dress with a V neckline and the crystal bead necklace he had given her so long ago when they were first married. With her lovely red hair piled on top of her head, he thought she had never looked more beautiful and elegant.

Katie looked so young and fresh. Her new dress was a shade of aqua that showed up her sparkling hazel eyes and was made of a clingy silky material that suited her tall slim figure. High heel sandals completed her outfit and the only jewellery she wore was her watch and a pair of glittering earings. She never bothered with make up ordinarily, but tonight she had gone all out, even to taming the riot of red curls that normally ran amok.

Jenny had been invited to join the celebratory dinner and arrived on the arm of Saul Jenkins to whom she had recently become engaged. He was a tall laconic country boy, easy going and friendly. His dark slicked down hair belied the fact his blue eyes and rugged good looks were used to roughing it outdoors on his father's horse agistment property just out of town. He had been her boyfriend ever since they left school.

Over dinner, they laughed and talked about old times at school and the horse ranch. Elizabeth was surprised there was no mention of this Mike that Katie had been mooning about for weeks. Whenever Elizabeth asked about him, Katie would say.

"Oh he's just someone I know!" Dan was not one for late nights, and since they were getting up early to give Katie her surprise next day, he suggested heading home leaving the young ones to stay and enjoy themselves.

As they were saying goodbye, Saul looked up and said to Jenny "There's Mike Wilson over there!" They all looked around and saw a group of young people standing by the bar. One well dressed young man with blonde hair was looking in their direction.

Saul raised his hand in greeting, and with a beaming smile the young man separated himself from the group and came over to their table.

Elizabeth shot a quick glance at her daughter, to be rewarded by seeing the brightest blush. The two young men obviously knew each other and as they shook hands, Saul introduced his fiance Jenny, Mr and Mrs Richards, and Katie. "Everyone, this is Mike Wilson, a friend of mine!"

Mike shook hands all round and when he got to Katie, he held her hand a little longer than a hand shake as he said,

"Katie and I already know each other." Elizabeth thought this would be a good time to leave, so she said.

"It's been very nice to meet you Mike. Dan and I were just leaving. I hope we'll meet you again."

They left as Saul was firing questions at Mike about how come he already knew Katie. Elizabeth gave a satisfied smile as she tucked her arm through Dan's and they went out into the night. Jenny and Saul were bringing Katie home, and it was after midnight when Elizabeth heard her come in.

Despite the late night, they were all up early next morning. Katie knew something was in the air as her parents had been acting mysteriously for the past week. Her mother especially was not good at keeping secrets. It had crossed her mind that since she now had her license, there may be a car sitting on the driveway. However this proved not to be.

The phone rang and Katie picked it up. Elizabeth heard her say, "Hi Terry!" A pause, then Katie covered the mouthpiece with her hand, turning to her mother, she said "Terry wants to know if I can give him a hand for an hour or so this morning." Elizabeth looked disappointed.

"We were taking you out for a special lunch. I've made the booking for 12.00. It was going to be a surprise, but if Terry needs you, we could leave now and still have time to get to the restaurant.

Katie spoke into the phone "O.K. Terry, I'll be there shortly." She hung up the phone feeling quite dejected. Going out to lunch with her parents was not the sort of surprise she had expected.

"Put your good clothes in the car and you can change at the ranch" called her mother. Pulling on her jeans, tee shirt and riding boots, she grabbed the hanger with her new dress and picked up her high heels, depositing them all on the kitchen table.

She went outside to give her dog a bit of a rough up, and shortly her parents joined her. She was surprised to find them so dressed up. Her father was even wearing his best suit.

What's going on?" she asked.

"Well!" said Dan "Your mother wanted to make this lunch special for your birthday. We'll take you out to the ranch and wait for you then we can all go to lunch."

On the drive out to the ranch Katie's thoughts turned back to last night at the pub after her parents had left. Mike had stayed with them the whole night. They laughed, danced and talked till late. She discovered he was twenty two years old, an only child like herself, and worked for his father.

Mr Wilson kept him busy, making sure he learned the business from the ground up as the stud would be his one day. To make the evening complete, it was he who had driven her home in the sports car.

She was still day dreaming when her father pulled up at the gate to the ranch and she noticed the sports car was parked in its usual spot in the shade.

Dragging her thoughts back to the present, she heard her father say "Take your time, mother has her book and I've got the paper, so go do what you have to do." Getting out of the car, she took the short cut through the horse yard rails and made her way to Terry's office. This time she wasn't surprised to see Mike sitting there with Terry.

She smiled at them both as she said, "What's up!" She sat down on the wooden box where the spare bridles and ropes were kept. Terry leaned forward in his chair as he said.

"Mike told me how upset you were when he mentioned that I was going to sell Manfred." She bit her lip, not wanting to hear what he was saying. "The buyer is coming to pick him up later today. I know how you feel about him, and I thought you might like to take him out one more time. You know, say goodbye and that sort of thing." She felt the tears start and just nodded her head as she hurried out of the office. She heard Mike call to her, "Hang on Katie, I'll walk down with you!"

She ignored him and started to run, not wanting him to see her crying again. Half blinded by tears, she ran into the tack room to get the gear, but his things weren't in their usual place. Mike caught up with her saying, "He's already saddled up Katie!"

She looked at him confused as he went on, "I was sure you'd take him out so I got him ready for you." She didn't know whether to thank him, or kick him so she just turned and strode out to the yard surprised to see Terry and her parents standing outside the rails.

She whistled up Manfred who came trotting over to her with a colourful lei around his neck. Before she realised what it was, the horse yard resounded with cries of 'Happy Birthday Katie!'

She stood there shocked, seeing the other volunteers, as well as Terry and her parents lining the rails, clapping. Again the tears flowed, this time with joy and amazement. Laughing and crying at the same time, she hugged Manfred who bobbed his head up and down as if he knew he now belonged to her. Standing just behind her, Mike was misting up too. When she turned and threw herself into his arms, laughing and kissing him, he was caught off balance, and they both went sprawling on the ground. Terry leapt the rails to help her up, whispering "Happy birthday kiddo. He's all yours!"

That was the start of years of happiness for Katie. She leased a paddock and agisted Manfred on the Jenkins farm. Elizabeth and Dan didn't see much of her these days. When she wasn't at work, she was at the farm. Mike would pick her up in the sports car, letting her drive occasionally.

Sometimes they would visit his parent's property, which she loved. It was set on a hill near the point of the peninsular. Magnificent views of the bays and the ocean shimmering in the sunlight could be seen from the Verandahs. The lush green grass highlighted by the white fence rails dividing the paddocks was so picturesque.

Between work and her friends, Katie's time was precious. Elizabeth enjoyed giving her a hand with the horse. Getting out in the paddock where the fresh smell of hay mixed with all the other horsey odours brought back happy memories. Some days she remembered the pain of her injuries, and silently prayed that history wouldn't repeat itself and Katie would always be safe.

One day when they were particularly busy at the clinic, Katie rang to ask her mother if she could go check on Manfred. The weather had been sultry the last day or two and now there was a storm brewing. Black clouds were gathering and she wanted to get the rain blanket on Manfred, but things had been so hectic at work that she couldn't get away. Tom said it was something to do with the weather. Elizabeth had been watering her pot plants but she was only too happy to go check on Manfred.

It was still warm so she didn't bother to grab her jacket. Calling out to Dan that she was going, she jumped in the car and took off towards the Jenkins farm. It was almost 5kms so by the time she arrived and opened the gate to drive through to Manfred's paddock, the sky was so black it looked like the storm would hit at any moment.

She whistled up Manfred and as he came trotting over to her the sky opened up and torrential rain began to fall. He was edgy and pranced around as she tried to buckle the straps of his rain blanket. She was soaked to the skin by this time. The wind had picked up blowing her wet hair across her eyes making it difficult to see what she was doing.

She almost had the last buckle fastened when a vivid flash of lightning, followed by a clap of thunder that seemed to rent the sky apart, spooked Manfred who reared up in fear, his front leg catching Elizabeth on the shoulder knocking her to the ground as he bolted, eyes rolling. The half done up rain blanket flapping out behind, spooking him all the more.

He bolted through the trees leaving Elizabeth rolling in pain and shock on ground that was fast becoming a mud hole. She tried to stand up but the pain was so severe that she crumpled to her knees.

Tears she couldn't hold back, mixing with the rivulets of rainwater running down her cheeks. Manfred ran until he reached the high fence around the homestead where he stood trembling, sides heaving, his breath coming in loud snorts.

Lon Jenkins had been standing on the verandah watching the storm and enjoying the much needed rain. Hearing what sounded like heavy horse breathing, he grabbed his raincoat and hat off the peg. Shrugging into the coat and pulling the hat low over his eyes he strode through the rain to check things out. Once he reached the gate, he could see it was Manfred very obviously spooked by the storm.

"It's alright boy," he said quietly. Reaching out his hand he slowly approached the horse uttering soothing words until he was close enough to pat him and reach across to fasten the strap on the rain blanket. "You did scare yourself didn't you old boy" he said as he led him under shelter.

Chapter 5

The last of the animal patients was finally seen to and Katie was able to go home. She had been worrying ever since the storm began, wondering if her mother had got out there in time to rug Manfred up. She grabbed her slicker that always hung in the office cupboard in case of rain. Summer storms like this one often blew in from the ocean venting its fury as it reached landfall.

She hurried the short distance home and was surprised to find no car standing in its usual place under the carport. Shaking the rain from her slicker on the back porch, she went in search of her parents.

She found her father in his study, having arrived home just before the storm began. Turning from his desk, he looked at her and exclaimed "My god girl, you look like a drowned rat, where's your mother?" "That's what I'd like to know" she replied looking worried.

"She was going out to put the rain blanket on Manfred for me. I hope nothings happened!" Turning back to his computer Dan said over his shoulder "She's probably having a cup of coffee with Mrs Jenkins and waiting for the rain to ease before driving home."

Katie had a bad feeling. It was not like her mother to stay and not let someone know what she was doing. "I'm going to phone and check if she is still there." Her father mumbled something as she left the study, and went back his work. In the kitchen, Katie picked up the phone and dialled the Jenkins number. After a few rings Mrs Jenkins answered. Katie could barely hear because of the rain pounding on the roof.

"Hi Mrs Jenkins" she said "This is Katie, is my mother still there?" Mrs Jenkins sounded surprised, saying "No dear, I haven't seen her at all." Katie sounding quite agitated said "But Mrs Jenkins, she went out to your place to put Manfred's rain blanket on him and she hasn't returned home yet. I'm really worried about her in this storm."

Hannah Jenkins was a kind motherly woman just turned fifty. She was concerned as she said "Try not to worry dear, you hang up and I'll get Lon on his mobile. He's gone out to check on one of the horses. He may know something." Katie hung up the phone feeling a big knot in her stomach. Something was wrong, she just knew it.

When his mobile rang, Lon was settling Manfred with some feed and a good rub down. Like his son Saul he was country born and bred to the saddle. Horses were his life. Never seen without his battered old akubra, his honest tell it like it is attitude endeared him to many.

Reaching for his phone, he said "Lon here!" he listened for a moment then exclaimed "What's that you say! Elizabeth? But I've got Manfred here. Oh my god, I have to go." Suddenly he realised why Manfred's rain blanket was dragging. He raced to the shed for the trail bike. Revving the engine, he went roaring up the track to Manfred's paddock. Cold fear ran through him as he sighted the huddled form of Elizabeth lying on the ground in a pool of muddy water. The torrential rain was beating down on her with its full force.

Skidding to a stop, he climbed through the fence rails and ran to her side. She was barely conscious and shivering violently. He quickly shed his coat, wrapping it around her as she muttered incoherently. Using his mobile he called for an ambulance and then tried to find out where she was hurt.

She could hardly speak because of the cold and shock but he managed to understand that it was her shoulder. She kept muttering M-Manfred over and over. He tried to comfort her saying that Manfred was alright, and was relieved when he heard the ambulance siren in the distance.

Once the ambulance left, taking Elizabeth to hospital Lon found himself shaking realising what a close call it had been. If Katie hadn't phoned looking for her mother this could have become a tragedy. Riding back to the house he thought about how easy it was to just assume that Manfred's blanket had come unbuckled causing it to flap in the wind thereby spooking him into bolting.

"Ring Katie" he said to his wife as he came indoors. "Just tell her that her mother has had an accident but she will be alright. Let her know an ambulance has taken her to the hospital and I will be there in about an hour." Hannah who had been anxiously waiting for him to come back was all questions.

"Just let me get out of these wet clothes and have a quick shower then I'll tell you as much as I know." he said as he headed for the bathroom. Hannah picked up the phone and dialled Katie's number.

Katie had been pacing up and down between looking out the window and straining her ears for the sound of the car. When the phone rang she jumped. Her heart began to pound as she picked up the receiver. She could hardly breath as she heard Hannah Jenkins voice. "You can stop worrying dear" she heard her say "Lon said to let you know your mother has had a slight accident and the ambulance has…

Ambulance!" screamed Katie "w what happened!" Hearing her scream, Dan came running from his study. She was breathing hard and panic stricken. Taking the phone from her hand he said "Hello, who is this, what has happened!"

"Dan this is Hannah Jenkins. It seems that Elizabeth had some kind of accident. I don't know any details but Lon found her and called the ambulance. He asked me to ring and let you know that she will be alright. He'll come to the hospital in about an hour and fill you in."

Thanking her, he hung up and turned to find Katie curled up in a ball crying "It's my fault! It's my fault! He reached down to cradle her in his arms uttering soothing words. He was at a loss when women cried, and never knew what to say. "What do you mean it's your fault," he gently asked. She was so distraught he had trouble understanding her words.

"I was busy today and I asked her to go and put Manfred's blanket on. That's why it's m-my fault. Helping her to her feet, he said "We don't even know what happened yet so don't start blaming yourself. Now dry your tears and we'll go to the hospital. Neither of them had given a thought to the fact that Elizabeth had taken the car. Fortunately Lon Jenkins arrived as they were about to leave.

"I passed your car on the way out" he said "It's inside my gate so it will be alright and we'll pick it up later. Manfred is fine so you don't have to worry about him and I'm pretty sure Elizabeth will be alright too."

They pulled up at the entrance to the E.R and before either could stop her, Katie was running through the doors looking for her mother. By the time Dan and Lon caught up, a nurse was directing Katie to a cubicle where they found a pale but weakly smiling Elizabeth propped up on pillows with a big sling on her shoulder and arm. "Thank goodness!" Dan muttered as they both stooped to kiss her. Seeing Lon standing in the background, Elizabeth stretched out her hand to him saying

"Thank you Lon, if you hadn't found me I don't know what would have happened." Lon shuffled his feet as he said "I'm not the one to thank, if Katie hadn't phoned Hannah looking for you I would have just thought Manfred had run spooked because of the storm and I wouldn't have returned him to his paddock in that deluge."

"Can you tell us what happened Elizabeth?" said Dan as they all looked at her expectantly."

"Well, it was no-ones fault really, just a series of events that started with the rain. I was fastening Manfred's blanket when a flash of lightning followed by a huge clap of thunder spooked him. He reared up in fright and his foreleg caught me on the shoulder knocking me to the ground. I tried to get up but the pain was so bad that I must have passed out.

I didn't know anything until Lon found me. The doctor said I was in shock and will need to have my shoulder x rayed to see if the collar bone is broken or just badly bruised. They've given me some pain killers so I don't feel too bad at the moment. I feel really tired though, must be the tablets." She closed her eyes and they kissed her saying they would come back later when she had rested.

Outside Lon asked Dan if he would like to drive back to the farm with him so he could pick up his car. Katie said she would stay at the hospital in case her mother woke up. After the men had gone she went to the visitors area to sit down. The storm was clearing fast as these summer storms do, and the sun was starting to shine through the clouds as the day was ending.

She found a quiet spot and pulled out her mobile phone. Since this whole horrible drama began, the only person she desperately wanted was Mike. Now as she dialled his number, the tears of relief surfaced and the moment she heard his voice, she broke down and the only barely coherent words he caught were accident and hospital. She heard him say "Hang on Katie, I'll be there!" and the phone went dead.

Mike had just finished a day's work with the horses. The storm had caused a few problems and he was wet through and covered in mud so had come in and showered. Recently he had moved into a unit of his own on the property and was about to get himself something to eat, when the phone rang.

Now he grabbed the car keys and drove the sports car at a reckless pace towards the hospital. Fear gripped his heart. He only knew that something terrible must have happened for Katie to be in such a state. It hit him like a brick, he loved Katie!

They had been friends for so long it took something like this to make him realise they were more than friends. He knew at that moment that she was his life. The car skidded to a stop outside the hospital and he ran inside suddenly scared of what he may find.

Inquiring at the desk, he was told that Katie was in the visitor's room and directed him down the hallway. He found her sitting alone in a corner of the room. She ran into his arms as soon as she saw him and burst into tears.

"Katie, whatever has happened!" he said trying to make some sense of things.

"I-It's mum" she said, her voice muffled against his chest. Holding her away from him, he looked into her tear filled eyes. "What about your mother" he said. "Stop crying and tell me what's going on."

Taking a deep breath, she said "Manfred was spooked by the storm and he reared up and bolted. His foreleg knocked her to the ground and now she might have a broken Collar Bone. I feel so bad, because I was busy at work and I asked her to go and put his rain blanket on. It was lucky Mr Jenkins found her and called the ambulance. It's all my fault." She started crying again and Mike felt like shaking her. "Where is your mother now?"

She sucked in a mouthful of air as she said. "She's had some pain killers and is sleeping. They will call me when the results of the x-rays come back"

"Well, that's good" he said, "now pull yourself together and wipe your face. It's not the end of the world, and it certainly was not your fault. I'm sure your mother will tell you that too." She started to disagree but he put his finger on her mouth saying,

"When you work with horses these things happen. I should know, I've been kicked and bitten so many times I've lost count. Now, where's your father?" Suddenly she saw Mike in a different light. He had calmed her down and taken control of the situation.

"He's gone with Mr Jenkins to pick up our car from the farm. He should be back any time now."

"Right" said Mike "we'll just sit here quietly and wait for him, and for the Dr to call you."

Sitting in the visitor's room with Katie, Mike found his thoughts swirling around in his head. He knew that he loved Katie, but he also knew she had a lot of growing up to do. While all he wanted to do was take her in his arms and tell her how he felt, he was mature enough to know he should back off and give her time and space. They were best friends, and that would have to do for now.

Dan and the doctor arrived together and there was relief all round when it was found that no bones were broken but Elizabeth had severe bruising of the bone and surrounding tissue. She was allowed to go home but had to rest after the ordeal and her arm and shoulder would be out of action for a few weeks. They all went in to see her as a nurse was helping her into a wheelchair to take her out to the car.

Although still pale and shaky, she gave Mike a smile and said how glad she was to see him, and thanked him for being such a good friend to Katie.

When they got her settled in the car, Mike thought this would be a good time to leave them alone. Saying he had work to finish before it got dark, he wished Elizabeth well and walked towards his car.

Chapter 6

With her mother out of action, most of the housework and cooking fell to Katie. With a full time job and her horse to look after there wasn't much spare time. Jenny, who had married Saul and was now pregnant, came to visit a few times. She and Saul had bought a house in town and were very excited about becoming parents.

Saul still worked on the farm with his father and often dropped Jenny off at Katie's where she kept Elizabeth company and helped out while Katie was at work. They chatted about this and that, with Elizabeth mentioning one day that they hadn't seen much of Mike lately. Jenny seemed surprised as he had been out to their place quite often.

"Oh I suppose he's been busy" she said. "You knew his parents went overseas didn't you?" Elizabeth didn't know and said "Well I guess that explains why we haven't heard his name around here as much as we used to."

The school year was coming to a close and that meant Dan would be home to take over some of the chores giving Katie a break.

Things were getting very busy at the clinic and Tom was becoming snowed under with work. One afternoon just before she left for the day, Tom asked her to come into the office. She sat down opposite him wondering what this was all about.

"Don't look so worried Katie, it's all good!" he said. She relaxed a little, thinking how tired Tom was looking these days. Running a hand through what was left of his hair he said.

"Katie I know you've always wanted to become a Vet and I think the time is right for you to think seriously about your future." She wondered where this conversation was leading, but sat quietly while he continued. "The business has become more than I can handle on my own and I've arranged for another Vet to come in with me.

If you are still keen to get your qualifications, this may be the opportunity for you to take up your university offer. With another Vet here, we could just hire a part time person to do your job."

She felt her heart thumping not knowing if she was being let go or what! "The decision is yours Katie so think it over, it's a chance to fulfil your dream if it's still what you want

." Coming out of left field like this was more than she could take in at the moment. It was something she had always wanted, one day. On the walk home, so many things were spinning around in her head. If she did this, it would mean leaving home as the nearest university doing Vet Science was interstate.

It would be bad enough leaving her family, then there was Manfred to think of and her friends, and what about Mike, he was her best mate, she could always talk to him about anything. She hadn't seen him since that day at the hospital so she would ring him tonight.

Arriving home, the first to greet her as usual was Prince who was always excited to see her. Today her mind was on other things and Prince barely managed to get a half-hearted pat. Her mother was sitting on the kitchen stool trying to manage with one hand. Normally Katie would rush over to help her but instead she just called "Hi mum" as she walked through to her room.

That's odd thought Elizabeth wondering if something had happened at work. She knew her daughter well enough to wait for her to say something and she didn't have to wait long.

"Mum" said Katie coming out of her room and sitting on the stool next to her mother, "What would you and Dad say if I took up my option to go to university and get my Vet degree?" This was the last thing Elizabeth expected to hear. "What's brought this up now, and how do you feel about it?" she said.

Katie relayed everything Tom had talked to her about. Elizabeth listened. "It's what I've always wanted," said Katie, "but there's so much to consider." Always the one with a cool head, Elizabeth said. "Why don't you help me get dinner and afterwards we can all sit down and discus the matter." Later when they were finished and the dishes done, Elizabeth said to Dan.

"Turn the T.V off dear, Katie has something she would like to talk over with us." He always liked to watch the news after dinner and thought this had better be important. Katie seemed to be nervous and he wondered what sort of trouble she had gotten herself into.

When he heard what she had to say, he was surprised, but pleased also, knowing it had always been her dream. They talked over all the pros and cons. particularly the part where she would have to leave home and only be able to come home at the end of each semester. The University of Queensland was offering the courses she needed but was over a thousand kilometers away. By the time they finished talking Katie was feeling excitement building. Jumping up she said "I have to ring Mike!"

She dialled his number and could hardly contain herself as she waited for him to pick up. When he did, she blurted out "Mike guess what, I'm going to Uni to do my Vet degree!"

"Hang on!" he said "Pass that by me again, only slowly this time!" She told him all that had occurred at work and how Tom had suggested she think about her future. On the other end of the line Mike was silent, He didn't know what to say feeling like someone had punched all the air out of him.

"Are you still there Mike?" He stared at the phone in his hand and said, "Uh yes I'm still here" This was the last thing he expected to hear, even though he knew it was her dream, he'd put it out of his mind.

"Well say something! Aren't you happy for me?" He changed the phone to his other hand realising how sweaty his palm had become.

"Of course I am" he muttered "It's just a bit of a shock coming out of the blue like that". Katy was on such a high she didn't realise Mike wasn't as ecstatic as she was.

"I know! I could hardly believe it myself when Tom suggested it, and I can't wait to see you and tell you all about it" She rattled on but Mike hardly heard a word his mind was running around in circles till finally he heard her say "I have to go Mike, there's so much I have to do, with Christmas coming and we're flat out at the Clinic. The semester doesn't start till March, so we'll have plenty of time to talk. Will I see you over Christmas"?

"I'll try" he said "but things are a bit hectic here at Wilton"

He replaced the receiver in a bit of a daze, trying to get a grip on what had just happened, or at least the parts he remembered hearing.

There was so much work to be done. With his parents overseas he was really struggling to get everything done on his own. Katy had been giving him a hand whenever she could, and at night he'd find himself thinking how great it would be having Katy with him always.

Now everything seemed to be changing, not that he resented her going to Uni and fulfilling her dream, but *his* dreams and plans seemed to be flying out the window at a great turn of speed.

The week before Christmas his parents returned from their trip exhausted but excited about where they had been, bringing presents and stories of what they'd seen. It wasn't long before his mother busied herself putting up the Christmas tree and decorating the house, while Mike and his Father saw to the horses and the property, getting everything squared away. Mike loved working with his Father. They both had the same love for the horses. Tony Wilson had begun 'Wilton Stud' from scratch and dreamed one day of passing it on to his son.

They had a wonderful Christmas day! In the afternoon friends dropped by and while they were being regaled with photos and a video of his parent's trip, Mike took the opportunity to visit Katie and her family.

Although he'd seen Katie a few times, the extra workload had prevented him going into town. He'd kept in touch about her Mother's health, and now looked forward to spending some time with them. Prince greeted him with loud barks as he drove up the driveway alerting all inside that someone had arrived.

Katie came out first to quieten Prince, and Mike was struck by how beautiful she looked. She was wearing the same lovely dress he'd seen her in on the night of her 18th birthday and he realised that he'd been in love with her since that night. Her short red curls had grown and now bobbed around her shoulders as she ran towards the car to meet him.

Her face was beaming. Stepping out of the car, Katie threw her arms around his neck. "Merry Christmas Mike, I'm so happy to see you and Mum and Dad will be too." Mike wished he could tell her how he really felt about her but he knew this was not the right time.

He gave her a hug and could feel his heart thumping as the perfume of her hair assailed his nostrils. "Merry Christmas to you too Katie" he murmured, not trusting his voice. She didn't seem to notice as she grabbed his hand and they walked towards the house. Reaching the front door, she squeezed his arm saying.

"I've got so much to tell you Mike." Prince was jumping all over him with excitement and Katie's parents were equally pleased to see him. Elizabeth was over her shoulder injury and gave him a quick hug as she went to put the kettle on. Dan shook his hand warmly saying "Good to see you my boy!"

Not being one for words, he was quite happy when Elizabeth came back with coffee and started plying Mike with questions about his parents and their trip.

"They're both well" he replied "At the moment they're probably boring the pants off their visitors with photos and the obligitory home video"

They all laughed, failing to notice Katie was trying to drag Mike away. She could hardly contain herself until they got a chance to slip outside and go for a walk. With Prince bounding alongside them, she began to fill in all that had happened since Tom had spoken to her at the Clinic. How she had talked it over with her parents and got their blessing.

She'd had to apply for an enrolment position at the nearest University that was offering the four year course. It was about a thousand kilometres away, and how if she was accepted she could only come home at the end of each semester. Mike walked along in silence, deep in his own thoughts.

"Well?" she said, stopping dead in her tracks, "tell me what you think!" He needed time to take it all in but looking down at her upturned face, so full of excitement and waiting for him to say something, all he could say was.

"I think it's great. It's a wonderful opportunity and it's been your dream for a long time. I say go for it".

"Oh Mike," she said, throwing her arms around his neck and kissing his cheek "I do love you and I'll miss you. You're my very best friend! Holding her close was torture as he whispered "and I love you Katie" It wasn't the same as *I'm in love with you* but it would have to do.

The rest of the day passed pleasantly. Katie was full of plans for the coming year. Elizabeth put up a great meal and afterwards they all sat outside in the cool evening just talking and laughing. It was a real family and Mike longed to be a permanent part of it. Later as he drove back to Wilton, his mind turned to his own life and what his future held. If only he had known what the fates had in store…

Chapter 7

Katie sent in her application along with her education reports including a glowing referral from Tom at the clinic. After the Christmas and New Year, she went back to work so Tom could take his break.

Although she loved working with the animals and their owners she often found her mind wandering to her computer, and rushed home each day hoping there would be an email answer about her enrolment. By the end of January she was becoming despondent. Finally, there it was! She had been accepted.

The confirmation and relevant forms etc. would arrive by post. Her screams could be heard by the whole street! Poor Dan, who was quietly working on his class lists for the start of the school year, threw them in the air with fright as Katie raced into the kitchen where Elizabeth was preparing dinner, nearly knocking her Mother to the floor as she spun her around shouting "I'm in! I'm in!

Eventually calm returned to the house as Elizabeth put dinner on the table but Katie's head was in such a whirl she couldn't eat a thing. Going to the kitchen, she picked up the phone and dialled Mike's number. She could hardly contain herself and waited impatiently for him to pick up. The phone rang a number of times before it was answered by Mr Wilson who said "Sorry Katie, he's not home."

Suddenly she felt bereft. Mike was her best friend and was always there for her. Her stomach seemed to flip over and she had to sit down not knowing if she was going to cry or faint. It was the strangest feeling. Elizabeth came into the kitchen and saw her sitting there with the receiver hanging limply from her hand.

"Katie, what's wrong?"

"What? Sorry Mum, nothing's wrong" she said as she stood up and replaced the receiver in its cradle

"I just phoned Mike but his father said he's not home and I had this weird feeling in my stomach. It must be the excitement! Where would Mike go at this time of night?" Elizabeth turned away to hide her smile.

In due course the official enrolment acceptance arrived together with all the information, class schedules, subject lists and possible student accommodation. This was food for family discussion. The semester was to begin mid March with orientation in February. Dan made the suggestion that Elizabeth go along, and while Katie did what she had to do, her Mother could do some sightseeing and enjoy a little break. Katie went along with the idea knowing that her Mother wouldn't worry about her so much if she knew where she would be. Apart from that it would be nice to have company on the plane. She had never flown before.

The next few days were taken up with work, booking flights and deciding what to take. Always at the back of her mind niggled the fact that Mike hadn't called her back.

Just on the off chance that Mr Wilson had forgotten to tell Mike, she phoned him again. This time his Mother answered, saying that he was busy out working with his father. Katie was left with the same feeling of abandonment and began to wonder if Mike was avoiding her. This was not like him at all.

On the day Dan drove them to the airport, the weather was overcast and raining but it couldn't dampen the excitement and anticipation. The fact that she hadn't heard from Mike was disappointing but it wasn't going to spoil this day she had waited so long for.

Mike had been distancing himself from Katie for the past week or so mainly because it was too painful to be near her, feeling as he did. He wanted her to live her dream, but selfishly hoped that she would miss him enough to realise they were meant for each other.

Through friends, he'd learned that she was leaving today for her orientation and that her Mother was accompanying her. He felt relieved knowing she was not flying alone. They would only be gone a few days, and in the meantime there was work to do on the Stud.

"Come on Mike" said Tony "With this weather blowing in we'd better check the horses"

Mike remembered a day just like this one, where the sky was overcast with a storm brewing. He'd never forget that panicked phone call from Katie at the Hospital. He got shivers just thinking about it. That was the first time he knew that he loved her. Life seemed to be changing and he didn't know where things would lead.

"Come on son, this isn't the time for dreaming" cajoled Tony. He was aware that something was going on with his son and Katie. He had been friends for many years with Lon Jenkins whose daughter Jenny was Katie's friend and her husband Saul had grown up with Mike.

"Better get the slickers on, that rain's not far off" he said as they headed for the tack room.

They worked hard for the rest of the day. While they were forking hay, Mike noticed his father seemed to be puffing a bit more than usual. "I'll finish this off Dad" he said "You fix up the saddles"

"Thanks son" said Tony with a sigh, "this holiday away has softened me up. I'll have to get back in condition."

Mike was throwing himself into his work in an effort to not think about Katie. Tony had passed over a lot of the work to Mike who just continued as he'd been doing while his father was away. A few days later they needed more supplies. Taking the old ute, Mike drove into town.

On the way his thoughts were consumed about Katie. He knew she would be back home by now, and he wondered if she had returned to work for Tom at the clinic. His heart ached for her and he knew he should have returned her calls but he was afraid that he wouldn't be able to hide his feelings for her and what if she rejected him! . . .

Pulling up in front of the vet clinic, he reached into his pocket for the list of supplies and felt his heart thumping in his chest. What would he say to her if she was in there? Jumping out of the utility he forced his unsteady legs to walk over and push the clinic door open.

"Oh! Thank goodness you're here" said Tom reaching over to grab the door. "Your mother just phoned and I'm afraid your father has taken ill and she needs you to return home at once." It took a moment or two for Mike to comprehend what Tom was saying, his mind had been in such turmoil. First it registered that Katie was not there, then he was questioning Tom as to what his Mother had said.

"Look Mike, all I can tell you is your Mother sounded most distressed and asked me to send you back home as soon as you arrived here."

"Thanks Tom," he said as he flew out to the utility and headed home his mind filled with dread as he remembered how tired and puffed his father had been when they'd been working

Approaching the stud, he heard sirens then the ambulance screamed past him turning into their driveway. Again his heart was thumping in his chest and fear gripped him. Pulling up behind the ambulance he raced into the house. His father was lying on the floor with the paramedics working on him.

"Oh my god Mum what happened!" he said

"I don't know" she said in a trembling voice "I made coffee and called him, then I heard a thump and when I turned around he was on the floor. Oh Mike I was so scared. He was unconscious so I just called triple O then I called you"

One of the paramedics asked some questions about his father's general health while the other one put an oxygen mask on Tony and they laid him on a stretcher to go to the hospital. Mike felt his mother shaking, she was close to tears. He didn't know what to do except ask what was wrong with his father. He'd never seen his father sick before.

"It may be his heart but we won't know till we get him to hospital" said the paramedic. "Would your mother like to ride in the ambulance with us?"

"You do that mum" said Mike "I'll follow you in the car"

When the ambulance left with the siren wailing, Mike slumped into the nearest chair, his heart thumping and a million thoughts racing around in his head. Gathering himself together he went out to the car and drove to the hospital.

Sitting in the waiting room it seemed a long time before the Dr came out and said "He's conscious now and stabilised We'll keep him overnight for observation and tomorrow I'd like to do an angiogram to check on the condition of his heart. If we find any blockages he could possibly require Bypass Surgery. Try not to worry though because he has always been healthy."

They drove home very much relieved having seen Tony before leaving the hospital. Mike's thoughts returned to Katie and it scared him to think how quickly things can happen that could change life forever. He resolved to tell Katie how he felt.

That night he phoned her, ostensibly to let her know about his father. Elizabeth answered the phone and was very concerned, enquiring how his mother was holding up and if his father had been ill beforehand. By the time he had explained everything to her and asked if Katie was there, he was disappointed to find she was not home. It seemed like fate was determined to keep them apart.

Katie was visiting Jenny and Saul. After a delicious meal they were sitting around the table chatting about her orientation visit.

"Have either of you seen Mike lately" she burst out. "I've tried phoning him a few times since we got back but he's never there and he hasn't phoned me. I feel like he's avoiding me. Do you think he's upset because I'm going to uni? He was really encouraging before I left, I just don't understand it."

Jenny and Saul stole a quick look at each other. They had seen Mike. He'd talked about how busy he'd been and how much he missed Katie. Jenny was about to say so when the phone rang. Getting up to answer it, they heard Saul say.

"What! My god what happened Mike? Katie jumped up, her heart racing! "Saul, what happened?"

Jenny grabbed Katie's arm and Saul waved her to be quiet as he listened to what Mike was saying. After what seemed to Katie an eternity, she heard him say "Yes she is here with us." Holding the phone out towards her he said "Mike wants to talk to you."

Almost snatching the phone out of Saul's hand, she cried "Mike! Oh Mike whatever has happened!" He explained as briefly as possible knowing how fond Katie was of his father. "We won't know if he will need heart surgery until after they do tests tomorrow. Katie I need to see you!"

With tears rolling down her cheeks she said "I need to see you too Mike, I've missed you so much!"

"I'm leaving home now" said Mike "I'll see you at your place." He just managed to stop himself from blurting out I love you Katie!

His Mother was calming down and having a cup of tea. She had overheard the conversation so when he said "Mum, I have to go into town. Will you be alright?"

"Of course" she said with a knowing smile "do what you have to do son, I'll be fine."

Mike drove in and out of town on a regular basis but until now he didn't realise how far it was trying to keep his speed in check, his mind was racing with what he was going to say to Katie. Finally her driveway came in sight and there she was, Prince at her side. He thought she had never looked so beautiful and he knew no words were needed. They flew into each others arms with love, raining kisses on each other.

"Katie I love you!" he said between kisses. "I think I've loved you forever, even when you hated me." Smiling through her tears she looked up at him, her face glowing with love as she said "Yes I did hate you once but I know now it was because I really loved you. I just didn't know it back then.

Prince started barking and jumping all over them feeling left out. It was unusual for him not to get the first pat. Looking at his expression made them both laugh. With arms around each other, and Prince trotting alongside they happily made their way into the house.

Elizabeth and Dan were very happy to see Katie and Mike so obviously in love but quite devastated at the news about Tony. Mike had to go over the details once again. "Oh Mike" said Elizabeth "How awful! As you say, tomorrow will tell the story. How is your mother coping is she alone out there?" With his arm still around Katie he said "Yes she is but when I left she was settling down with a cup of tea.

She told me to go!" He shot a loving look at Katie as he said "She knew I had something special to do in town."

Moving to put the kettle on Elizabeth said "Your father has always been a strong healthy person, so try not to worry until we know if there's something to worry about. Now, what about you two" she said, giving them both a big hug. "Dan and I have had our suspicions that something was going on and we're so happy for both of you aren't we Dan!"

Being a man of few words Dan stood up and reached out his hand to Mike. "Good to see you son" he said shaking Mike's hand. He was not a demonstrative man so the hug he gave his daughter meant the world to her.

"We're just going for a walk mum" said Katie. She almost pushed Mike through the doorway in her hurry to get him alone. Out of sight of the house Mike folded her in his arms murmuring words of love. Katie was ecstatic and couldn't stop kissing him. "I can't believe I've been in love with you all this time" she said between kisses. "I didn't realise it until I couldn't get you on the phone and I thought I had lost you.

"Katie my darling" he said, "I'm sorry I scared you but the truth is I was avoiding you." Pulling back so she could see his face, her expression was one of puzzlement. "I don't understand, why would you do that?" Smiling gently down at her upturned face he said "because I've been in love with you for so long that being near you was becoming unbearable. I've wanted to take you in my arms and tell you how I felt but I was scared. I thought you may just look on me as your best friend, and I couldn't bear to lose the woman I love and my best friend at the same time."

Katie gave a big sigh and hugged him tighter. "Yes" she said. "You are and always will be my best friend who I just happen to be in love with." They kissed long and passionately each feeling their heart soaring with love.

After a while they came down to earth and Mike said "Let's go out to my place. We can check on mum and then spend a romantic evening alone." "Mmm sounds wonderful" sighed Katie as they got into the car.

Chapter 8

The next day time seemed to drag as Mike and his mother waited for the Doctor to call with the results of Tony's angiogram. There was always work to be done with the horses so Mike was kept busy but his thoughts were with Katie. He could hardly wait to be with her again.

When the phone call came it was not good news. Tony was very lucky the paramedics had worked so fast and got him to hospital quickly. The test showed that he had blockages and would require open heart surgery as soon as possible. That afternoon Mike drove his mother to the hospital then went to pick up Katie.

Seeing Tony lying in the hospital bed looking pale and tired was quite a shock. He was a popular member of the community and word had spread rapidly. When they arrived home, the phone hardly stopped ringing. Later Mike drove Katie home and they talked a lot about their future. Since discovering their love for each other they had been floating on clouds but all this had put a damper on things.

"Oh Mike" said Katie "I love you so much, and now I'm all mixed up!" She snuggled up to him and he wrapped his arms around her. Kissing the top of her head he said "Talk to me darling, what's mixing you up." Turning brimming eyes to him she said "It's my University course. I don't want to leave you now, and the semester starts in a few more weeks. I can't bear the thought of being so far away from you and now there's you father" . . .

"I'm sure my father will come through this ok. He's a tough old bird," said Mike. As for university, the thought of you going away tears me up too, but it's been your dream for so long and I know you'd regret it if you gave up now." They kissed and the clouds of doubt rolled away.

A few days later Tony Wilton went in for surgery. It was a stressful wait until the call came to say the operation was a success and he was in recovery. After five days he was released from hospital under strict instructions to rest, do the prescribed exercises, and no work with the horses for at least three months.

This meant Mike had his work cut out running the stud and listening to his father's instructions about everything. "I don't know how he thought I managed things while he and mum were overseas" he said to Katie.

She had been spending as much time as possible helping out. They loved working together, sneaking little romantic moments when-ever they could. The spectre of her going away hung over their heads. One night a few days before she was due to leave they were together in Mike's unit, loving each other and talking. She looked at him in shocked surprise when he got down on one knee and took her hand declaring his love for her and asking if she would marry him.

For several moments unable to utter a word, she saw the love in his eyes and knew in her heart how much she loved him and wanted to be his wife, but not right now! His expression turned to puzzlement as he looked into her eyes now glistening with tears.

"Katie darling, what's wrong?" he uttered, totally confused. Finding her voice she said "Oh Mike, I love you so much and I do want to marry you, but what about my becoming a Vet!" She could see her life shattering in a thousand pieces and didn't know what to say.

"Katie, my darling Katie," he said as he got up and sat beside her on the couch "I do tend to blurt things out at inappropriate times. I want you to be my wife so much, I was panicked by the thought that we only have a few days left before you go away. I'm so sorry I scared you!"

Folding her in his arms he said "Of course I didn't mean right now! Locked in an embrace they talked for a long time about their future life together. Both agreed to leave things as they were. Just knowing they would marry when the time was right was enough for now.

Elizabeth and Dan put on a going away get together for Katie so all her friends could say goodbye and wish her well. It was a happy and also sad affair. Everyone could see how much in love Mike and Katie were, especially Jenny and Saul who worried how Mike would cope with Katie being away for four years.

Jenny was due to give birth in a few weeks and was not really into partying at the moment so giving Katie a hug and whispering "I'll keep in touch. Good luck with everything and be happy!" Saul hugged her saying, "The time will pass quickly you'll see."

Katie didn't see at all, it was starting to get too much and she was having second thoughts about whether she had made the right decision.

Looking around for Mike, she saw him with a group of their friends. Excusing herself, she grabbed Mike's arm dragging him outside into the garden where she threw herself into his arms as the tears flowed.

"I can't do it!" she sobbed "I know it's what I've always wanted but now I don't want to leave you, and I won't be here when Jenny gives birth and I'll miss Manfred, he can tell I'm going away!. Oh Mike, what am I going to do?"

Holding her tight he said "You leaving is killing me too! We talked about this remember! When you settle in I'll fly up every second weekend and we'll keep in touch every day. Once the semester starts and you get into it you'll realise it was the right thing to do. I'm so proud of you. We have a wonderful future to look forward to at the end of all this. I can't wait till we're married my darling!"

As the plane taxied down the runway these words echoed in her mind. Last night they had spent together in Mike's unit, and the memory was fresh in her mind. They had declared their undying love for each other and planned how it would be when they were married. She hadn't wanted to go home, but her flight was to leave early next morning. Mike also had to leave early to attend the horse sales so hadn't been able to see her off.

After a three hour flight, someone from the university was there to meet her and two others who had been on the same flight. They were a married couple. Introductions were made and the three hit it off right away. Katie felt less lonely as they chatted while waiting for the mini bus that was to take them to their accommodations.

Her new friends were Simon and Glenda O'Brian who managed a large property in northern Victoria owned by Simon's father. Glenda was medium height with a mop of unruly brunette hair. She was a friendly and chatty down to earth farm girl, while Simon was tall and muscular from years of farm work and didn't see the need to say much. They were both 25 years old and their plan was to open a veterinary clinic when they graduated.

Chapter 9

Tony Wilton continued to recover well from his surgery. He was frustrated that he couldn't get out to his beloved horses, and was driving Mike and his mother crazy with all his instructions. It got to the point where they talked to his doctor to find when he would be well enough to travel. Then they set about planning a surprise trip to get him away for a while.

Saul had been giving Mike a hand, but with the imminent arrival of their baby he didn't like to leave Jenny on her own for long. A week later their little girl was born. They named her Kaitlin after Jenny's best friend.

Saul was so over the moon he was very little help to Mike, who thought he would have to get someone in to help run the stud. With two new foals born a day apart, it was getting a bit too much to handle on his own.

He felt bad that a month had passed since Katie left and although they kept in touch by text, he hadn't been able to keep his word about visiting every second week-end. She replied that she understood how busy he had been, and how excited she was about becoming an honorary aunty. Everything was going well and she was enjoying university life, but missing him terribly. The next week Lon Jenkins offered to come and help out, allowing Mike to fly to Brisbane

Exiting the plane, he scanned the arrivals lounge until he saw Katie. Spotting him at the same time, they rushed into each others arms. "Oh Mike! I've missed you and I've got so much to tell you!" she said.

Looking at her flushed face and sparkling eyes he could hardly believe how much she had changed in such a short time. She was wearing jeans and a little white strappy top that showed off her recently acquired suntan and he couldn't take his eyes off her. Gathering up his over-night bag, Katie led him by the hand through the terminal and out to the car park. The weather was quite warm and he was regretting wearing his jacket.

She paid the parking ticket machine saying "come and meet my baby!" A little red VW was tucked in between two big 4WD monsters. Squeezing his hand she said "Isn't he beautiful? I bought him cheap from one of the graduating students. The Gatton campus is a fair way from the main university and I needed transport."

As they drove out of the car-park Katie said "Do you remember Simon and Glenda, the couple I told you about who came up on the same flight as me?" He nodded, and she rattled on "Well they're both doing the Bachelor of Veterinary Science the same as me, and have rented a three bedroom house just off campus. I'm sharing with them."

He looked sideways at her in surprise. She didn't seem to notice and went on "It's just an old Queensland style house, high set with a Veranda all around. It came furnished so we didn't have to buy anything. I know you are going to like them, they are such a fun couple."

He sat silent as they drove out of the city looking around at this unfamiliar place and thinking who is this vivacious chatty girl! He knew he loved her, but she seemed so different from the nervous Katie who left six weeks ago.

On the outskirts of the small but pretty township of Gatton was the Agricultural Campus of the University of Queensland. Passing the entrance gates, she pointed out different areas to him until they pulled up outside the house. It was quite different from the usual houses found in Victoria and had an enormous mango tree almost blocking the view of the house.

Unwinding his 193cm frame Mike climbed out of the little 2 door car. Grabbing his bag and jacket from the back seat, he followed Katie up the steps into the house. They were alone at last.

Dropping his bag on the floor he took her in his arms and they kissed long and hungrily. Holding her away from him, he looked down on her lovely face and marvelled at the change he saw. Gone was the uncertain young girl he had fallen in love with, she had suddenly morphed into a beautiful woman so desirable he couldn't bear to let her go.

She snuggled up and laughingly said "If you keep looking at me like that I'll have to kiss you to death. I'll show you where to toss your bag." Pointing to the spare room, she said "You can sleep here, if you want to." Then giving him a sultry look, she said "my room is just next door!"

His hormones had been raging whenever he was near her since her 18th birthday that night at the pub. Now at twenty five he was on fire and would have raced her off right there and then but for the slamming of the wire door and a woman's voice calling "We're home!"

The mood was broken. Grabbing his hand Katie led him into the kitchen where Glenda was dropping bags of groceries onto the table. Before Katie could get a word in, Glenda said.

"Hey you two!" She gave Mike a wide smile as she said "I'm guessing you're the wonderful Mike." Reaching out to shake his hand she said

"Good to meet you at last, you're all she ever talks about." Katie gave a wry smile and Mike noticed she was blushing. "Simon will be in soon" said Glenda. "Typical male, he thinks he heard a strange noise in the car engine so he's under the bonnet trying to figure it out! I'm for a coffee, what about you two?"

Without waiting for an answer, she set about clearing some room on one end of the table to put out four mugs then put the kettle on. Just as the water came to the boil, the wire door slammed and a very hot and dishevelled Simon came in.

At first he didn't notice Mike until Glenda said in her down to earth way, "Simon, meet Mike."

Startled, Simon reached out his hand apologising for the state he was in "Mike." he said "pleased to meet you. I'd better go wash up." Over his shoulder he said to Glenda "it was just a couple of loose wires."

They took their coffee out to the veranda where the mango tree threw a cooling shade in the late afternoon. Mike felt very comfortable. They talked easily about their lives finding common interests. He wasn't left out when they spoke of their studies as it involved animals particularly horses.

He found himself wanting so much to be married to Katie. He thought about the times they worked together and of the camaraderie they had shared and he wanted it all. He tried to put it to the back of his mind knowing how much Katie wanted these qualifications.

The week-end was wonderful but unsettling to both of them. Knowing they would be parted again next day, made their lovemaking bitter sweet as they clung to each other not wanting the night to end.

For Mike the flight back to Melbourne seemed endless. Although he tried to think about his father's health and the fact he would have to get someone in to help with the workload, he couldn't get Katie out of his mind.

For Katie the long drive from the airport back to Gatton stretched before her in a blur. She was suddenly doubting herself. Did she really want to be a Vet?

The more she thought about it, the more she wanted to be on that plane going home with Mike. She loved him so much it was painful. She had visions of the beautiful property and working together with Mike.

Before she realized it she was parking the car under the Mango tree. Her housemates were having cool drinks on the veranda watching her as she dragged herself up the steps looking like she'd been crying.

Glenda got up to get Katie a cool drink whilst shooing Simon away. He started to object, but the look his wife gave him was enough to send him scurrying inside to watch television. Katie flopped into a chair as Glenda brought out her drink. Staring into space as she sipped her drink.

Katie was hardly aware as Glenda kindly murmured "I know you miss him, but he loves you and he'll come back soon."

Turning to Glenda with tear filled eyes, Katie tried to find the words to describe how confusing her life was becoming.

"I know he loves me and I love him so much, but that's not the problem." she said twisting the glass in her hand. "I've always wanted to be a vet, but now I'm having doubts. I can't explain it to myself but it hit me all of a sudden when Mike left. Becoming a vet always seemed to be the most important thing in my life but I know that's not true any more."

She looked imploringly at Glenda waiting for her more experienced advice. Ever practical Glenda stood up saying "I think we need coffee then we'll talk." Coffee was her answer for any problem that arose and this seemed to be one of those times.

The aroma of coffee wafted by Simon's nose as he stood up to go back outside. Glenda quickly stopped him. "No sweetie, you have your coffee in here" she said "Katie and I need a little girl time." Since he'd been living in a house with two women he was getting used to being odd man out. Glenda gave him his coffee then carried the other two mugs out to the veranda. Sitting opposite Katie she said.

"Sweetie, Simon and I are in this together, so I can only imagine what it must be like for you to be separated from Mike. It must be hell! Having said that, could it be that you're very homesick and that is clouding the issue?

Katie sat stirring her coffee as she said "You're right about that. I am homesick. I'm missing my family and friends but it's more than that. Is becoming a vet what I really want or was it just a girlhood dream. I love animals particularly horses and working with Tom at the clinic always inspired me." Glenda nursed her coffee and was silent She knew there was more to come.

"Mike and I have been best friends since my 18th birthday and he has always encouraged me to follow my dreams, even after we'd fallen in love. I'll be 21 soon and I've grown up a lot. Am I doing the right thing? Am I letting everyone down, or am I letting myself down, I don't know! It's why I'm so confused."

Looking at her friend's downcast face Glenda was at a loss to know what to say. Eventually she said "I really don't know what to tell you except to say look into your heart and be honest with yourself. Try to relax and tomorrow you may see things more clearly."

After a sleepless night tossing and turning Katie was no clearer in her mind. She was moving like a zombie as she wandered into the kitchen which led Simon to comment "You look like hell!" Glenda gave him a push that almost sent his face into his breakfast. The surprised look on his face made both girls laugh and Katie's gloomy mood evaporated.

Later as they had coffee on the veranda before going to their classes Katie said "I think I may have worked out a solution but I need to check out a few things.

Chapter 10

Back in Victoria, the first thing Mike noticed was the cold weather. This time he was glad of his warm jacket. His parents were happy to see him back and he was glad to see his father looking like his old self. No-one was happier to see him back than Lon Jenkins who had been bearing the brunt of Tony's frustrations. Shaking Lon's hand Mike said with a grin, "Sorry mate! I know he's a bit of a pain at the moment. He's usually great to work with but the doc said no work with the horses for another two months. Let's hope we can all survive till then. I plan on getting some-one in part time to give me a hand until he recovers."

Next day he went to town for supplies and called in to see Katie's parents letting them know she was doing well. Elizabeth was glad to see him and asked lots of questions.

While waiting for his order to be made up, he took a run out to the Trail Riding Ranch to have a chat with Terry. It was fairly quiet this time of the week. A few volunteers were working around the place. He climbed through the horse yard rails and made his way to the office where he found Terry on the phone. They were old friends and Mike poured himself a coffee from the machine while Terry finished up his call. "Mike!" said Terry with a wide grin as they shook hands. "Haven't seen you in a while, how's your dad?"

"He's doing well, driving mum crazy trying to get him to obey doctor's orders. He's not to go back to work with the horses for another couple of months." Terry laughed as he said "I've known him a very long time and patience is definitely not part of his agenda."

"That's one reason I've come out to talk to you." said Mike. "Things are getting very busy and I'm finding there's just not enough hours in the day to get everything done on my own. Katie was working with me before she went to Queensland and it was great. Now I need some-one to come in even part time, to give me a hand until the old man is back on deck.

I was hoping you might be able to recommend one of the volunteers who could be interested in some work experience. I'd pay them of course." He drained the last of his coffee as Terry thoughtfully skimmed through the pages of his volunteer book. Scratching his head, he murmured a few hmm's then looking up at Mike he said," there is one here who might be interested but I'd need to sound her out first. If you could leave it with me for a couple of days" . . .

"Thanks mate" said Mike. On his way home, having picked up the supplies he thought about who it was Terry had in mind. Hoping it would be someone experienced in the type of work required, he put it to the back of his mind and concentrated on happier thoughts.

Katie did a lot of soul searching over the next few weeks and decided to work through this first semester. To Glenda, it appeared Katie had settled down until one day while they were having breakfast, she suddenly announced "I'm not going to be a vet." Her housemates looked at her in astonishment. "What? both chorused, "When did this happen!"

"Well," said Katie "I've been giving this a lot of thought and instead of doing the full veterinary course, it would be in my better interest to concentrate on equine studies as part of the Bachelor of Science program. What do you think?"

Glenda smiled as she said "Well sweetie, I think you've already made up your mind!" Getting up to make coffee, she said over her shoulder. "Sounds like a plan, but are you sure you've thought it all through?" Taking her coffee to the table, she sat nursing her cup as she said thoughtfully

"I suppose, with you and Mike living and working on a Horse Stud, unless you are fully committed to becoming a Vet, it could be a bit of overkill don't you think, when you have a Vet clinic already on your doorstep."

Katie felt a weight lifting from her shoulders. Having her thoughts verified by Glenda, it was a relief to feel a calm pathway in her mind instead of the constant maelstrom racing around in her brain preventing her from concentrating on her studies or sleeping properly.

"I'll talk with the course co-ordinator" she said as she put some bread in the toaster and poured herself coffee. "I'm not going to say anything to Mike until I've worked it all out, then I can surprise him when I go home at the end of this semester" she said.

Little did she know something was about to happen on Wilton Stud that had the potential to change her life forever.

A few days after he'd spoken to Terry at the Trail Riding Ranch Mike received the phone call he'd been waiting for. Not one to beat around the bush, Terry simply said "I've got the girl for you mate! Her name is Erin Roberts eighteen years old. The family runs a small adjustment property over at Mornington so she knows her way around horses. I'll send her to see you tomorrow and you can take it from there."

Next morning quite early Mike heard the sound of a car coming up the long drive towards the house. Not wanting his parents disturbed, he waited outside on the pebbled driveway as a big white 4wd wagon skidded to a stop scattering pebbles all over the garden bed. Thinking this must be his possible assistant, he was surprised when the door opened and a pair of long shapely legs emerged followed by a very attractive blonde haired girl wearing a tee shirt and cut-off jeans. The only other indication was the pair of well worn riding boots adorning her feet. Jumping lithely down from the vehicle she approached Mike with hand outstretched.

"Hi!" she said with a wide smile, "I'm Erin. Terry sent me over, are you Mike?"

It took him a second or two to find his voice. Shaking her hand, he apologised for his hesitation saying "Yes I'm Mike!" With a laugh she said "Not what you were expecting huh!"

"I don't know what I was expecting." he said "I'm just looking for someone to give me a hand with the horses until my father is back on the job. Terry recommended you so that's good enough for me."

"I don't mind hard work" she said as he led her towards the stables. She hardly drew breath, talking all the way "I've been helping my dad since I was little. There are two girls in my family, my sister is younger than me so dad treats me like the son he never had."

Mike found that hard to believe. She chattered away and he found her very likeable. He hoped she could work as well as she could talk.

By mid morning they had achieved quite a lot and he found she was as good as her word. They took a break and went up to the house where he introduced Erin to his parents. Her arrival on the stud was timely since Tony had finally agreed to take a recuperating holiday though no definite date had been set. He had been so cranky lately using the excuse that his constant input was needed. Now that it looked like Mike would have some help around the place, he might agree to take a break.

Erin was very comfortable when meeting new people. She had plenty of confidence and in the short time it took to have her coffee and snack, they had all learned her life story and how happy she was to be able to fill in for Tony until he was back in the saddle (her words).

Mike said he was satisfied with the way she worked and she could start the next day. Waving goodbye to her, the wagon disappeared down the driveway in a cloud of dust and flying pebbles, leaving Mike and his parents slightly shell shocked.

"Well son!" said Tony "She's a firecracker all right. Watch out she doesn't have you working for her!"

Mike laughed as he said "Don't worry dad, she talks a lot but works well and certainly knows her stuff." A couple of weeks later Tony and his wife went off on the long awaited holiday.

Erin had started work and was coming three times a week. It took the first week to catch up on the backlog. After that everything fell into place and they developed a comfortable working relationship

Mike was missing Katie. He thought about how well they had worked together and the love they shared. He knew it wasn't possible for him to make another trip to Queensland for a while so he had to be content to share text messages with her and dream of holding her in his arms every night. He let her know that Tony had at last relented and agreed to take a short trip now that someone was there to give a hand until he got back.

Katie messaged back how much she loved and missed him, not mentioning anything about the doubts she'd had and the plans she was making about the change to her course. There were only a few more weeks left of this first semester. She'd had a talk with the co-ordinator, who was sympathetic and gave her much the same advice as Glenda.

Go home at the end of semester and really think it through. If she was homesick, a visit home may put everything into perspective and she could continue her course. If not there was always the option to defer or give it up.

This was good advice and she felt much happier now everything was clear in her mind. She returned to her usual cheerful self, much to the delight of her housemates. The semester was coming to an end and with only a few more weeks before they all went home for a short break, excitement was beginning to seep into the house. Glenda and Simon planned to relax on the farm while Katie could only think of being with Mike again.

"What about your parents eh!" teased Glenda "I guess they'd like to see you at least once," she said with a laugh. Simon had to add "Are you going to let Mike know you're coming? He might have to hide all those other girls ha ha."

"Oh very funny Simon, how would you like to wear this spaghetti!" Katie said. They were cooking dinner between then and the mood was light and happy. That night Katie lay awake for a long time thinking about home, her parents, friends, and most of all Mike. Simon's joke about other girls was disturbing. She had been in love with Mike for so long it had never occurred to her that there may have been other girls in his life. What if he had met someone while she had been away?

This thought scared her so much and it wouldn't go away! Next morning she was up early to send another text message to Mike assuring him of her love and how she couldn't bear it if he wasn't in her life. The next few weeks would seem to stretch out forever. Her cheerful mood seemed to have evaporated much to the concern of her friends.

When Mike received the text he was puzzled. Why would she mention about him not being in her life! He had been up half the night with a mare who was about to foal so didn't have time to answer. Putting the phone in his pocket, he would reply tonight. Erin arrived just as he reached for the thermos of coffee he'd made before coming to the stable.

"Good timing" he said "You can take over while I take a break. She's reasonably calm and I don't think it will be long now."

Erin had a way with the horses, much like Katie he thought.

"You are such a good girl," crooned Erin as she knelt in the hay stroking missy's nose. Turning to Mike she said "I'm so glad I got here in time, even though I've worked with horses nearly all my life, this is the first time I've seen a foal born. It's so exciting! Looking up at Mike, she seemed to have a glow about her and he realised this kid as he thought of her, was in fact a very beautiful young woman.

Finishing his coffee he knelt down beside her and together they worked until finally Missy had her foal. Mike had been through this many times before but to see this miracle through Erin's eyes filled him with renewed awe. Silently they watched the little colt stagger and fall as he tried to stand. It was a reverent time for Erin, and Mike couldn't take his eyes off her. Suddenly she seemed to realise where she was and jumping up threw her arms around his neck and he saw the tears sparkling in her eyes. Holding her away from him Mike said.

"It's the best feeling isn't it!" Suddenly things were back to normal and Mike went about tending to Missy and her foal while Erin chattered away in her usual fashion.

The next week Mike had to go up country to tend to some business negotiations, representing his father. This would be a two day meeting with him being away overnight. Erin was a quick learner and he had faith in her that she could look after thing while he was away. He had been living in the main house while his parents were away so he made the suggestion that Erin might like to stay in his unit while he was gone.

She was a bit surprised, but since she didn't have much money and the way the wagon guzzled fuel she thought it a good idea. The day before he left she arrived bringing her overnight bag. He showed her around the unit, and they discussed the daily work and what he wanted her to do while he was away.

Next morning she waved him off and set about her work.

Chapter 11

In Queensland thing were not going well for Katie. It all started with the text she had sent Mike when she was feeling depressed and insecure. He didn't text back immediately as he usually did. That night he did answer, but it was brief saying that he'd been really busy he loved her and would text again when he had more time.

This was so unlike him. It caused her to imagine all sorts of things and although his later messages declared his love and how much he missed her, she couldn't seem to shake this awful feeling that something wasn't quite right.

That night she decided to phone him. They had agreed to text each other rather than phone unless it was an emergency. The house she shared had no phone so thinking about how much credit she had on her mobile phone, she dialled but got the recording that the mobile she had called was switched off. This was not right! He never switched his mobile off. She would phone his unit. This bad feeling was making her feel sick.

After a few rings it was picked up and a cheery female voice said "Helloo! This is Erin, is that you Mike?

Katie froze! The phone fell from her hand, this was a nightmare. Picking up the phone and with her voice barely audible she muttered "No this is Katie, is Mike there?" "No," came the cheery reply "He's gone up country for a few days. Can I take a message?"

Her knuckles white from the pressure of holding the phone Katie managed to say "W-Who are you?"

"Oh I'm Erin, Mike and I are running the Stud while his parents are away. I'm living in his unit. He'll be back in a couple of days. Can I tell him you called?"

Sinking to the floor Katie weakly replied "Er no, I'll catch him later." Still holding the phone, she curled herself into a ball of abject misery where Glenda and Simon found her. Rushing to pick her up and prise the phone from her clenched hand Glenda turned to Simon saying "get a blanket and a glass of water." As he rushed off she gently eased Katie into a chair saying "talk to me, whatever has happened?" Turning dry unseeing eyes to her Katie murmured "I've lost him."

"What are you saying!" said a bewildered Glenda "Who's lost who? She took the blanket Simon had just brought in and wrapped it around Katie. Simon handed her the glass of water saying "What's going on?" He never could figure women! Going out to the veranda he muttered "a man's better off watching TV."

Glenda was wise enough to not ask questions knowing it would all come out in good time. Katie's voice was barely a whisper as she cried "what am I going to do!"

Glenda stood up and took charge in her usual way saying "First thing you're going to do is go to the bathroom and splash some cold water on your face, while I put the kettle on. When you come out, we'll sit down with some coffee and you can tell me the whole story." Katie stood up and walked as in a dream toward the bathroom.

Glenda gave a big sigh as she filled the kettle. Entering the kitchen Simon repeated his earlier question "What's going on?" Putting the kettle on, she turned to Simon giving him a big hug saying "I love you Simon!"

"What the heck was that for!" he said. This was getting too confusing even for Simon.

"I'll explain it all later" she said as Katie came into the room looking like a ghost. Her face was pale and her eyes red from crying. Although she was very fond of her young housemate, Glenda sometimes wished she was more mature without all these insecurities.

Aware the big 'girl' talk was about to happen, Simon made a quick exit with the excuse he had 'things' to do.

Having made the coffee, Glenda handed a mug to Katie saying, "Let's sit outside and talk about what has you so upset." After a slow start Katie recanted everything that had happened since Simon's joking remark, and about the phone call that seemed to confirm all the awful thoughts she'd been having.

Glenda made a mental note to kill Simon, then she said to Katie "I'm sure there's nothing to worry about. Everyone can see how much you and Mike are in love! You said yourself his text messages are filled with love. I think you could be reading more into something that could have a simple explanation."

"Yes but what about this Erin person, who is she and why is she living in Mike's unit?"

"I can't answer that" said Glenda "The only thing I can suggest is that you go home and sort everything out. We don't have any more important lectures, so rather than let this eat you up for the next week, go now and find the answers for yourself. Glenda could sympathise with Katie remembering how she had felt when someone had misinformed her that Simon had been seen out with another girl.

Finishing her coffee Katie realised what a wonderful friend Glenda was. Being a few years older, she always seemed to know the right words to say and her reasoning always made sense. Getting up and hugging her friend she said

"Thanks Glenda, I'm sorry to always lay my problems at your feet. I don't know how I would have survived this semester without you and Simon"

"Yes well I wouldn't mention Simon at this point" said Glenda as she picked up the empty mugs and followed Katie into the house.

That night Katie phoned her parents telling them she would be home in a couple of days as soon as she could get a flight. They were very excited and said they would pick her up at the airport.

"If you see Mike" she said "Please don't tell him I'm coming home early. I want to surprise him"

It was two days before she could get a flight back to Melbourne. It gave her time to tie up loose ends with her course. It was left open as to her to return. Simon drove her to the airport with Glenda lending her support and reassurance. After they left her, all the doubts and worries returned.

She was excited to be going home. Her parents were at Tullamarine Airport to meet her and it was a happy group who made the rest of the journey. It was late in the day when they reached home. Prince was waiting with tail wagging as soon as he heard the car. When Katie stepped out, he went wild with delight almost knocking her over. She roughed him up then followed her parents into the house. Immediately a sense of peace came over her.

"When are you going to let Mike know you are home." said her mother.

"Oh" she said "I just want to settle down and relax tonight. I'll drive out there in the morning and surprise him."

Elizabeth and Dan looked at each other as Katie dragged her bag into her room. This was not at all what they expected. Did something happen with the romance? They had been surprised it wasn't Mike who met her at the airport, but knowing Katie of old, they refrained from asking questions.

Katie was torn between her desperate need to see Mike and rush into his arms with love, and the thought that if he had found someone else, he might be distant and that would destroy her.

Chapter 12

After a restless night she emerged to eat breakfast. Elizabeth covertly watched her, looking for some signs of a problem but she chattered away like her old self. She got up and washed her own dishes, a habit learned while house sharing.

Giving her mother a hug, she said "Can I borrow the car? I want to go out and surprise Mike." Elizabeth smiled as she handed over the car keys. "Say hello to Mike for us" she said as Katie left with a big smile on her face.

The smile disappeared as she climbed into the car and set off for Wilton Stud. Her heart was thumping uncomfortably in her chest as she turned up the long drive to the main house. Already parked there, was an unfamiliar white 4WD wagon.

With her palms starting to sweat, she walked purposefully toward the stables. Hearing music which was most unusual, she followed the sound to find a young girl mucking out the stable. Her back was turned as she raked the hay giving Katie the opportunity to observe her without being seen.

She seemed quite young, wearing jeans and tee shirt with her blonde hair tied up in a pony tail. Could this be Erin? Katie coughed and called hello? Startled Erin turned and Katie could see she was older than she looked from the back. Turning off the music she said "Sorry, I didn't hear you. Can I help you?"

"Is Mike around?" Katie asked in as normal a voice as she could manage.

"I'm Katie"

"I'm Erin" she replied "Mike's around here somewhere" she said "I'll call him on the radio." Katie hadn't noticed the two way radio hooked on Erin's belt.

"Are you there boss" she called, "Yes but I'm busy. Is it important!"

"I'm not sure" she replied "I'll ask. She said her name's Katie" a pause then, "boss are you there? huh that's weird, must have dropped out" she said.

Katie had to admit to herself there was something likable about this girl. Erin looked outside and said,

"Oh here he comes and he's sure in a hurry!"

Katie looked and her knees went weak as she saw Mike running towards her arms outstretched. "Katie!" he yelled. Then she was in his arms being spun around, her feet off the ground. In between kisses and laughter he exclaimed "I didn't expect you for another two weeks, this is the best surprise ever!"

Looking over his shoulder Katie saw Erin smiling but bewildered. Mike noticing Erin for the first time, put Katie down but keeping his arm around her, said "Sorry Erin I'm being rude. This is my beautiful Katie who I'm going to marry. if she'll have me!"

"Wow boss!" she said "No wonder the radio went dead, it really was important"

For Katie, the world exploded in a kaleidoscope of colour and sunshine. She had never felt such happiness mixed with relief and love, it was almost too much. She couldn't stop the tears as they rolled down her cheeks, alarming Mike who thought something was wrong.

Seeing his stricken look, turned the tears to rather hysterical giggles. She had been so stressed out and worried until this moment. Suddenly her legs gave way and but for Mike's strong arms holding her she would have collapsed to the ground.

Standing by with a rather bewildered look on her face, Erin leaned on the rake she'd been using and kicked at some hay, not knowing quite what to do as Mike gathered Katie up preparing to carry her to the house. As if realising Erin was still there, he gave her a big grin.

"Sorry Erin, I'm not usually this scatty, take the rest of the day off. No, take the rest of the week off! I'll catch up with you in a few days." Katie was on her feet again, and Erin watched as they walked towards the house, arms around each other.

She felt a little envious seeing how much in love they were, and dreamed of finding that kind of love herself one day. Up at the house the young lovers talked, loved, and talked again. There was so much to catch up on and plans to make. When it was time for Katie to head home, Mike accompanied her ostensibly to officially ask her father for her hand in marriage but also because he couldn't bear to let her go.

This was such an exciting time for everyone. Elizabeth was already making plans for the wedding. The Wilsons wouldn't be home for another few weeks but Mike knew his parents would be over the moon when they heard the news. After a lot of discussion listing pros and cons about Katie's course, she decided to go back next semester and finish the year. With her qualifications in Equine health and Stud Management under her belt, they could seriously start planning their future lives together.

At the start of the new semester it was a very different Katie who met up with her now very good friends Simon and Glenda at the airport. Glenda was amazed at the change in Katie. From the worried teary person they had farewelled a few weeks ago, she had become a happy mature woman bathed in the glow of love.

On the way back to Gatton, they talked about their time at home and their plans for the future.

Chapter 13

The rest of the year passed swiftly. They all studied hard and when Katie's 21st birthday came around, Mike arrived bringing Elizabeth and Dan, along with his parents for a surprise visit. Katie had been expecting Mike, but not the families so it was torture for her not to be alone with him. Along with Glenda and Simon, they all went to the local club for a celebratory 21st dinner. To mark the special occasion they had all dressed up. The excitement was palpable during the meal, all knowing what was coming. Katie felt the breath leave her body as Mike got down on one knee, producing the little velvet box from his pocket Taking her hand in his, their eyes locked and the rest of the world vanished.

"Katie," he said "I love you so much!" Opening the little box, he withdrew the beautiful diamond ring they had both chosen when she had gone home. "Katie, I can now ask you officially. Will you marry me?"

"Oh yes darling yes, yes, yes!" she replied as he placed the ring on her finger. As if the whole party were holding their collective breaths, applause and congratulations burst forth around the table. Eyes shining with unshed tears Katie looked around at all the people she loved especially Mike who was also her very best friend.

Once home again, Elizabeth was in her glory arranging everything for the wedding as per instructions from the bride and groom to be. Katie wanted Jenny as her bridesmaid and Glenda as her matron of honour. Mike had asked Simon to be groomsman and of course he asked Soul, who had been his best mate all these years to be his best man.

The big day finally arrived. The wedding coach was pulled by Manfred who was less than impressed by the white feathered plumes attached to his bridle and kept shaking his head in an effort to dislodge them.

In the church Elizabeth sat in the front pew with Mike's parents. When the sound of the wedding march began so did her tears. Katie looked beautiful as she came down the aisle on the arm of Dan who looked so handsome and proud. When he had done his duty, he came to sit with his wife and in his quiet fashion, handed her the tissues.

After the ceremony, with the guests gathered around outside congratulating the happy couple, Elizabeth heard a small sweet voice calling "horsey, horsey!" Looking around she saw Jenny's daughter Kaitlin holding her chubby little arms outstretched towards Manfred. In that instant she knew in her heart there was indeed something mystical and magical between a girl and a horse.

The End

Lightning Source UK Ltd.
Milton Keynes UK
UKHW011828260522
403577UK00001B/112